Boo-a-bog
in the Park

This book is dedicated to
The Children's Hospital for Wales,
and with love to Gabriel

Published in 2016 by Pont Books,
an imprint of Gomer Press, Llandysul, Ceredigion SA44 4JL
in support of the Noah's Ark Appeal.

ISBN 978 1 78562 169 7

A CIP record for this title is available from the British Library.

This book is published with the financial support of the Welsh Books Council.

Printed and bound in Wales by Gomer Press,
Llandysul, Ceredigion SA44 4JL

Boo-a-bog in the Park

Lucy Owen

Illustrated by Andy Catling

Pont

Down in the park
where the children roam free,
Tom sat wondering . . .

Why don't they play with me?

Boys running wild

Girls shrieking loud . . .

too busy to notice him
alone in the crowd.

Then . . .

. . . a ***rumble***

in the bushes

to the treetops

branches ***shake!***

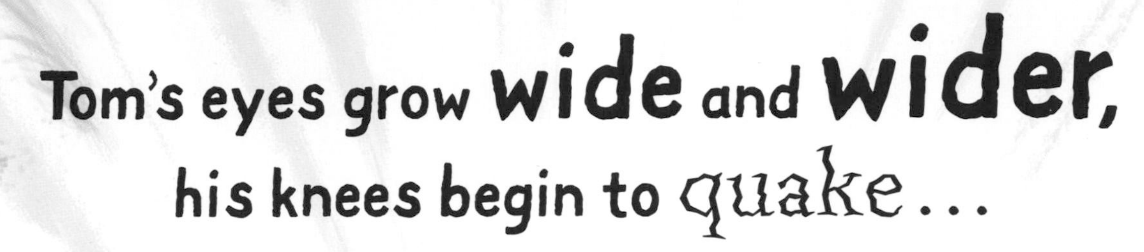

Tom's eyes grow **wide** and **wider**,
his knees begin to quake...

Scaly horns, great brown hooves,
a matted, furry tum;

a pool of drool upon the ground . . .

Oh now's the time to run!

Two crusty claws poke through the shrub –

'Does no one else here see?

a **monster**, staring from the bush! And he's . . .

Smiling

– straight
at me!'

The widest smile, the toothiest grin
from tattered ear to ear,
a mop like moss upon his head –
eyes crinkly, kind and clear.

'I'm a Boo-a-bog.
I'm a Boo-a-bog.
I'm a Boo-a-bog,
I'm a Boo-a-bog,
don't you know . . .
Poke

and we can be together
wherever you may go.'
Sniff
Yuck

'Let's play crazy
fun park games!'
the jolly monster cries.

Now Tom's heart begins to lift
as he looks in Boo-a-bog's eyes.

'I've a Boo-a-bog beside me
I've a Boo-a-bog by my side.
I could do most anything –
take anything in my stride.'

Hide and seek,

crawl and creep,

give each other

a **fright!**

Two best friends chase their dreams
until the fading light.

puff
puff
puff
puff
puff
puff
puff
puff
puff
huff
puff
puff
puff

'I've a Boo-a-bog beside me
I've a Boo-a-bog on my side.
I can do most anything –
take anything in my stride.'

Sam sees Tom laughing loud -
and wants to be his friend!
They run, they jump
they skip about -
The fun will
never end.

More children now beside them –
Not hard making friends, after all!
Just what Boo-a-bog
always wanted –
Tom happy,
standing tall!

Quietly Boo-a-bog turns away,
not sad, just time to go.
A gentle **smile** upon his face,
his great big heart a-glow.

'Goodbye Boo-a-bog, you made me strong.

You gave me courage too.'

‘Oh no,’ came the voice of his fuzzy friend.

‘It wasn’t me.

It was you.’

Lucy Owen is a television presenter and journalist. She is an Ambassador for the Noah's Ark Appeal, which raises money for the Children's Hospital for Wales. Her profit from this book will be donated to the charity. Lucy lives with her husband Rhodri and son Gabriel in the Vale of Glamorgan.

This is Lucy's first ever published book for children and she hopes that you really enjoy it!

Andy Catling is a professional scribbler and splurger of pictures and has illustrated for publishers around the world. He works in traditional mediums and digital wot-nots to make artwork with a rigorous mangle-like process. First he draws a picture. Then he rubs it out and draws it again. He colours using watercolour, pencils and ink, sniffs it, screws it up and starts over. The digital work process is much the same but without the sniffing. (All digital artwork smells of screen wipe.) Andy lives in the UK and thinks he is a pirate.

Boo-a-bog
fun and games

1. How many children are in the park with Tom on the first page of the story?

2. Where was **Boo-a-bog** hiding?

3. What colour is **Boo-a-bog**'s nose?

4. What did Tom do when he first saw **Boo-a-bog**?

5. What's the first game that Tom and Boo-a-bog play together?

6. What is the name of Tom's new friend?

7. Think of three words to describe Tom and three to describe Boo-a-bog.

8. Why not draw your own imaginary monster friend?

What is your monster's name?

What does it like to do?